Pirate Party

by Llinos Mair

Wenfro

O! Gwyn ein byd
- a gwyrdd!

Pont

What a windy day it was! Mam-gu Iet-wen looked up at the sky.

Why is Branwen, the white crow, flying on such a windy day?

Suddenly, she heard a scream coming from the garden.

1

Mam-gu Iet-wen hurried to see what was wrong. Owen was rubbing his head while Olwen looked on excitedly.

What did Olwen have to show Mam-gu Iet-wen?

'Open it, Owen. What's the message?' asked Mam-gu Iet-wen.
Very carefully, Owen took out the rolled-up paper.

The children read the message carefully. It was an invitation — an invitation to a party.

Come to the beach party — as soon as you can. B.

I wonder who sent it?

B? Who on earth is B?

'A party!' said Mam-gu Iet-wen. 'I like the sound of that.' Mam-gu Iet-wen had a very good idea who 'B' was.

4

Owen and Olwen ran inside to get ready.

But there was no sign at all of the friendly scarecrow.

Suddenly the sky lit up with all the colours of a rainbow.

Oh no! Morning rainbows bring more rain.

Mam-gu Iet-wen looked worried. She hoped it wouldn't rain on the party on Aberawen beach.

There was no need to worry. It was Ceinwen, the butterfly, in colourful party dress. Just like the children, she couldn't wait for the beach party to begin.

You're dressed like a rainbow, Ceinwen.

It's going to be a bright and colourful party.

It certainly was, thought Mam-gu Iet-wen. She loved the bright blue sea, the golden sand and the frothy white waves at Aberawen.

At last everyone was ready to set off, but Mam-gu Iet-wen had one eye on a dark cloud that was hovering above them.

Off they went to the mystery party. The children were still trying to guess who B might be.

On the beach, Bwgi-bo was getting very excited. He had been planning this fancy dress party for a long time and had collected driftwood for a pirate-ship on the rock.

I'll be like Barti Ddu, the fearless Welsh pirate.

He was so glad that Branwen had helped him deliver the invitation to Iet-wen and very happy that she had returned to help him again.

But then, Bwgi-bo and Branwen found something terrible.

Bwgi-bo watched helplessly as a crab and other tiny creatures scrambled out of the inky water, escaping the sticky black ooze.

He peered into the rockpools. The seashells and the seaweed were black as night. Well, this dirty beach was no place for a party, thought Bwgi-bo.

We'll need help!

He sat in his special ship to have a proper think about this.

Branwen was feeling helpless. What was spoiling their lovely beach?

Branwen had an idea. She took a piece of driftwood and began to write a message in the sand before joining Bwgi-bo.

Suddenly, a huge wave broke onto the rock. Bwgi-bo, Branwen and the driftwood ship were drenched in smelly, black water. Branwen's message was washed away.

Now you really do look like Barti Ddu!

Branwen flew high into the sky to try and dry herself.

15

Just then, Branwen spotted her friends coming along the clifftop. Mam-gu Iet-wen, Owen, Olwen and Ceinwen had arrived at last.

Look! A crow!

No, it's a black and white magpie – one for sorrow.

Mam-gu Iet-wen and Olwen didn't realise that the bird flying above them was Branwen, the white crow.

Mam-gu Iet-wen spotted Bwgi-bo on the rock below. He was waving his arms and jumping up and down like a dancing pirate.

The black seaweed stuck to Bwgi-bo like stringy black hair and a ragged beard.

Suddenly, a ball of black feathers fell just passed Mam-gu Iet-wen's nose. It made a tiny croaking noise as it dropped through the air.

That sounds like Branwen's voice!

Ceinwen rushed to find out what could have happened to Branwen, the white crow.

Down on the beach, Bwgi-bo had seen Branwen struggling to fly. Her wings were thick with black ooze and they just wouldn't work at all.

Branwen landed right in Bwgi-bo's arms. That was lucky!

Mam-gu Iet-wen reached the beach and hurried over to Bwgi-bo and Branwen. Everyone looked very worried.

Oh dear! This is oil.

Mam-gu Iet-wen realised that Bwgi-bo wasn't in fancy dress after all. He was covered in dirty oil. Poor Bwgi-bo!

The children inspected the beach. They found a little crab that was covered in black spots near the rocks.

'It's trying to escape from the oil,' said Owen.

The sky darkened and by now there was a strong wind blowing. The windmill on Bwgi-bo's hat whizzed around. And finally the rain came. Huge droplets fell.

The wind blew harder, and everyone watched as, wave after wave, the water tried to wash away the black streaks on the beach. What a black day it was.

Suddenly, Ceinwen, the butterfly, had very important news to share with everyone. She explained that the oil had spilled from a ship out at sea.

Thank goodness they managed to repair the ship.

'Some good news at last!' said Mam-gu Iet-wen.

'Every last drop of this oil will have to be cleaned or it will harm the wildlife!' explained Mam-gu Iet-wen.

Before she could answer, Mam-gu Iet-wen remembered about poor Branwen. 'Come!' she said. 'We must hurry back to Iet-wen at once!'

On their way home, the children asked Mam-gu Iet-wen all about oil. 'Oil is a dirty fuel that is taken from the earth,' explained Mam-gu Iet-wen.

Our house gets heated from the ground!

And we get electricity from the sun and the wind.

'That's excellent!' replied Mam-gu Iet-wen. Bwgi-bo jiggled excitedly as the twins mentioned clean green energy.

As they made their way home Mam-gu Iet-wen explained that they would clean Branwen's feathers very carefully.

Bwgi-bo will need a long soak in the bath.

And a good scrub!

'Taking a photo of Branwen and Bwgi-bo, before and after a bath would be a good idea,' said Owen. He wanted to send the pictures to the local paper.

As soon as they got back, Mam-gu Iet-wen began to clean Branwen's feathers. She filled an old milk bottle with special soap and water from the well and pierced the cap to create a special shower.

Branwen had found her voice!

'Let's have our party here, in our garden,' suggested Mam-gu Iet-wen once the cleaning was done. The sun was shining once again and everyone was safe.

A surprise party after all...

Hooray!

'We're pirates on board the Iet-wen ship,' said Owen. 'And Bwgi-bo is our captain!'

The Aberawen Disaster, with pictures of Branwen and Bwgi-bo, was front page news.

Everyone laughed.

First published in 2016 by Gomer Press, Llandysul, Ceredigion, SA44 4JL
www.gomer.co.uk

ISBN 978 1 84851 863 6
ISBN 978 1 84851 931 2 (ePUB)
ISBN 978 1 84851 943 5 (Kindle)

Part funded by the Welsh Government as part of its Welsh and bilingual teaching and learning resources
commissioning programme.

Ariennir yn Rhannol gan
Lywodraeth Cymru
Part Funded by
Welsh Government

Printed and bound in Wales by Gomer Press, Llandysul, Ceredigion, SA44 4JL